THE WOLFSONG SERIES

The WOLF'S SONG

SAVIOUR PIROTTA

ILLUSTRATED BY
DAVIDE ORTU

Contents

The Islands
(The Orkneys)

Wolf's village
(Skara Brae)

New Island
(Rousay)

Great Island

The Island
of Red Cliffs
(Hoy)

Seal Island
(Flotta)

The
Whispering
Stones
(Stone Henge)

The Cave of
Dancing Animals
(Lascaux, France)

Chapter 1
Dreaming of Monsters

I sat perched on the edge of a cliff, my feet dangling high above a shimmering sea. Shadow, my trusted dog, snuggled beside me, his muzzle resting on my lap. My friends, Crow, Sting and Rain, had gone to bed in a cave nearby. The warm air was heavy with the smell of wild flowers, making me drowsy. But I was determined to stay awake. This was a moment to savour and enjoy, a moment I wanted to remember for the rest of my life!

I'd just come to the end of another perilous adventure, one that had taken me far from my home in the north, across land and sea to a small, mysterious island at the centre of the world.

My best friend Crow and I had come here in pursuit of a boy from my own village. His name was Rain and he'd been my bitterest enemy ever since I can remember. He'd taken the most precious thing I'd ever owned—a bird-skull amulet whose special seeing-dreams sent me warnings about the future. With the help of Crow and another girl we met on the island, Sting, I had managed to get my amulet back.

I'd forgiven Rain for stealing it. It was clear that his quest for power had left him even more powerless. With forgiveness came peace in my heart. I was looking forward to the future with hope and a newfound confidence, something that I have not always had in life.

I am training to be a shaman, for I believe the spirits have given me the gifts needed to help and guide people to a better, more contented life. Many shamans have a special song that is uniquely their own. They sing it when they need help from the spirits. My song sounds like the howling of a wolf. Truth be told, I am still in the process of learning it. The special song is not taught to you by a teacher or a shaman but by something deep inside you; the same mysterious thing that makes you want to help people rather than become a wealthy or powerful person.

I sang my song now, howling like a wolf at the bright moon. Singing reminded me of who I truly was: Wolf! A boy from Great Island, far to the north where the cold never leaves, not even in summer. Bathed in moonlight, the sea swirling far below me, I let the song flow through me. I thanked the spirits for helping me retrieve my bird-skull amulet, and for making up with my former enemy, Rain.

I was about to ask them for help with the long journey back home, when the amulet hanging inside my tunic twitched. My fingers flew to my chest. It twitched again, harder this time, the curved beak scratching my skin. It was a sign that the amulet was going to send me a seeing-dream.

A ripple of excitement went through me. I pulled out the amulet and held it up in the moonlight. It was a bird's skull with a small beak and two small pebbles for eyes. Normally these were a dull black but now they were gleaming, as if they had come alive. The amulet swung back and forth on its string. The eyes bore into me and I felt them drawing me in...

A moment later, I felt myself falling off the cliff. I plunged into the sea feet first, like a flint-tipped spear hurled at a deep-water fish. The warm water closed over my head and I sank deeper and deeper, through a forest of swaying brown seaweed until I landed gently on my knees in soft sand. Scrambling to my feet, I saw crabs and little fish skittering away from me.

In front of me stood the ruins of a sunken building the likes of which I had never seen before. The roof was held up by neat piles of round stones placed one on top of the other so that they looked like polished tree trunks. I guessed it was a temple of some kind because there was an altar right in the centre of it. Above it, the roof had a wide crack; forked like a bolt of lightning.

As I watched, a greenish glow appeared in the sea behind the temple. It bobbed slowly, coming closer and getting brighter until I could make out that it was a gigantic sea-creature with a strange light glowing out of its forehead like a lamp. The beast had multiple flailing arms that reached wide to curl around the stone tree-trunks of the ruined temple.

The creature seemed to be ill or injured because it crawled along with difficulty. Its eyes, sunken into its flabby, round head, were glassy and unseeing. Dark spittle—or perhaps it was blood—oozed out of its mouth. Had it just fled from a losing battle with some other monster?

I heard the creature moan in pain. Then it shook, gasped and collapsed onto the floor, taking the altar down with it. At once, a shoal of small fish darted into the temple. They were hideous things with pointed teeth like my mother's bone needles. As one, they descended on the injured creature and sank their gnashing teeth deep into its flesh.

The monster roared feebly. It tried hitting out but there were too many fish and its tentacles were too weak. The strange light on its forehead flickered, dimmed and went out. The hideous fish scattered and melted away.

Daring to move closer, I could see there was nothing left of the pitiful monster but a pile of bones on the temple floor. This was more of a nightmare than a seeing-dream. What could it possibly mean?

But wait—now another light was making its way towards the temple. It was brighter than the creature's green glow, and bluish-white in colour. As it came closer, it split into a swarm of smaller lights that floated in the water around me.

I recognised them by their wispy tentacles: they were jellyfish. I had seen many of them in the sea near Great Island, although none glowed like this.

They danced gracefully round the creature's bones, reaching out with their shimmering tentacles. They seemed to me almost like human shamans performing a sacred ritual. Their dazzling light moved along their tentacles and into the scattered bones.

Propelled by this magic, the scattered bones of the dead sea-creature joined with one another to form a skeleton again. Glowing flesh appeared to cover them and within moments a living creature rose majestically from the temple floor.

It was the same monster as before, with the glowing light on its forehead and far-reaching tentacles. But it was also a new creature, younger, stronger and healed from its wounds! Its skin glowed with the same bluish light as the jellyfish and its eyes sparkled with life.

They looked directly at me.

The monstrous tentacles reached out towards me, wrapping me in their squelchy brilliance. I was lifted right off my feet and—a moment later—I woke up.

Shadow was growling beside me, his tail thumping on the dusty ground. A voice spoke out of the cave.

'Wolf? Are you still out there?' Crow appeared at the mouth of the cave. 'Why don't you get some sleep? We have a busy day tomorrow.'

ChapteR 2
The Sacred Pool

Puzzling though my seeing-dream was, I had not much time to try and figure out what it meant. The moment I got under my furs, I fell into a deep sleep and I didn't wake up again until morning sunlight was streaming into the cave.

Sting and Crow had already had breakfast and were sitting at the mouth of the cave, restringing their bows.

'Good morning,' said Sting. 'Would you like some fruit-stew? There's some in the bowl.'

'Where is everybody?' I asked as I helped myself to the stew, rich and fragrant with spices.

'They're visiting relatives,' said Sting.

I carried my bowl over to the mouth of the cave. 'I thought the grown-ups on this island never went out during the day.'

'The caves here are connected with tunnels,' explained Sting.

'Just like the houses in my village,' I said. 'Where's Rain?'

'He's gone with my parents,' chuckled Sting. 'He was very keen to tell everyone about our adventure in the Forbidden Temple and the important role he played in it.'

I smiled to myself as I thought how Rain would enjoy telling the story. Some parts of him hadn't changed after all. Perhaps they never would.

'We stayed behind so we can talk about what we're going to do next,' said Crow.

I sat down beside her in the sunshine. It was still early in the morning but it was already hot, the air clear and without any hint of mist.

'The boat will come to fetch us in a few days,' I said. 'All we need do is keep low so that Starlight and his men don't find us.'

Now that I had my bird-skull amulet back, I was keen to start on our journey back. Moon, my mentor and Rain's father, was waiting for us at the sanctuary of the Whispering Stones.

'But we can't leave without knowing what Starlight and his men are going to do next,' argued Crow. Her dark eyes flashed in the sunlight. 'They might take their revenge on Sting and the rest of the people on the island.'

'We can take care of ourselves, don't worry,'

said Sting. 'I'm more concerned that they might come after *you*.'

I looked from her to Crow. 'After us?' I said.

'They were planning to sacrifice Rain, weren't they?' explained Sting. 'My father says the followers of She Who Sleeps never sacrificed people, only animals which they later cooked and shared in a common feast. Starlight and his men are not like that. They're really bad. They might chase you just to get their revenge.'

'You're right,' I said. 'We need to find out what Starlight means to do next. But how are we going to do that?'

'There's a secret waterfall with a sacred pool not far from the temple of She Who Sleeps,' said Sting. 'Legend has it that the Goddess herself bathed in it at the dawn of time and that some of her powers remained in the water. The priests of old used to go there after the midday meal, to shelter from the fierce sun and to cleanse themselves before the afternoon ritual. The chief priest even used to spend the night there, praying to the Goddess. Starlight and his priests might do the same. We should pay them a visit. Perhaps they might discuss their plans and we'll learn something.'

'But will they talk about secret plans out in the open?' I asked.

'The pool is in a very sheltered spot,' said Sting. 'The path there is narrow and the priests can keep an eye out for anyone coming. But I have my own way there that they wouldn't know of.'

After our own midday meal, Crow, Sting, Shadow and I crept out of the cave, Sting leading the way. The heat was stifling. Sweat poured down my face and dripped off my chin in a steady stream. It was quiet, as if everything on the island was sleeping through the heat. Not even an insect buzzed, which was a blessing. I didn't want Shadow to bark at anything.

We made our way down a cliff and across flat land blanketed with ripened crops. Back on Great

Island, the wheat would not be ready for harvest until the dark days of autumn. Here, though the stems were thin and brittle, the crops were already tall enough to hide in. We wormed our way through them towards the sacred pool.

Beyond the wheat fields, we came to rocky ground covered in thorny bush, and then to a grassy meadow covered in wild daisies. With the temple of She Who Sleeps to our left, we crept through the flowers until we found ourselves in a shady glade. Round stones and shells hung from the branches of trees, tinkling against each other in the afternoon breeze.

'They are meant to be magic amulets,' whispered Sting. 'The priests of old hung them there to protect the Goddess while she swam. It is said that if you came too close, the sound of those stones in the wind would stay in your ears until it drove you mad. Even now, you'd never find a Bee Child coming this close to the sacred pool.'

'But *you're* not scared,' said Crow.

'I have heard the stones and shells tinkling in the breeze many times,' giggled Sting. 'I'm not mad yet. But listen…'

I heard the sound of familiar voices against the splash of water. Crow beckoned us forward and we hid behind an enormous boulder. Peeping round it, I could see Starlight and three of his men sitting near the waterfall, their legs dangled in the sacred pool. It truly was a magical spot; the water in the pool a bright green, and the rocks around it shiny and smooth.

The priests were talking in loud voices but the sound of the waterfall was drowning them out.

'We need to get closer,' whispered Sting. 'Come with me.'

Crow and I followed her round the boulder and in a wide circle until we were right on the other side of the pool. The ground here was muddy with spray from the waterfall. We crouched behind a thorny bush and listened. Starlight's voice was now loud and clear. It seemed we had arrived in

the middle of a conversation about us.

'Believe me, I'll get my hands on that boy if it's the last thing I do,' growled Starlight. His voice was so angry it sent a shiver down my spine. Poor Rain! Only a few days ago I would have gladly given him up to Starlight myself, but now all I wanted to do was help protect him.

'I agree,' said one of the other men, a thin fellow with enormous hands. 'It shouldn't be too difficult to find him on this small island. We'll get the guards to turn the whole place upside down if we have to.'

'And when we catch him…?' asked a third man.

'We force him to wake up She Who Sleeps. I reckon if he came all this way to retrieve the bird-skull amulet from the other boy, he must be the true boy from the old prophecy. He's the one we want.'

Hearing those words, my blood turned to ice. Starlight and his men were not after Rain.

They were after me!

CHAPTER 3
Sting's Plan

In truth, it had never occurred to me that I might become Starlight's next target. I turned to speak to Crow but she put a finger to her lips and shook her head.

Starlight's men put on their sandals. 'We shall prepare the temple for this evening's ritual,' said the one with the big hands. 'Will you be joining us?'

'Yes,' said Starlight. 'Light the fire at the altar. But leave me now. I need to bathe in the sacred waters.' He waded deeper into the pool while the men gathered their belongings and left in the direction of the Forbidden Temple. We waited until the coast was clear, then returned to Sting's cave.

Sting's parents and Rain had returned, bringing gifts of honey and bread from their relatives. Sting explained what we'd heard at the sacred pool.

'I won't let them lay a finger on Wolf, don't worry,' said Crow fiercely. Shadow growled and bared his teeth to show he would protect me from Starlight too.

'But all we have to do is hide till your friend's boat comes to fetch us,' said Rain. 'Then we'll *all* be safe.'

'I'm afraid leaving the island won't necessarily solve your problem,' said Sting's mother. 'What's to stop that evil priest coming after you in a boat of his own? He might still want to sacrifice you, Rain. And if he and his men manage to force Wolf to utter the spell and wake up She Who Sleeps, her anger will destroy the entire island.'

'They will *never* force me to recite that spell,' I assured her.

'She's right,' said Sting's father. 'Those men are cruel and heartless. They *will* make you recite the spell if they catch you.'

'So what do we do?' I cried.

The situation was hopeless. There seemed no way of escaping Starlight and his wretched priests. Sting paced around the cave, her hands behind her back.

'How much time do you need to get safely back home?' she asked at last.

'It will take at least five moon cycles before we reach Crow's island,' I said. 'I should be home by the start of winter.'

'Then all we have to do is prevent Starlight and his men from following you until then,' she cried. 'Listen, everyone. I have a plan…'

A bright moon hung low in the sky as Crow, Rain, Sting and I crept out of the cave again, taking digging sticks and Shadow with us. The sky was littered with more stars than I had ever seen. I thought about whether, if he was awake, Moon might be looking up at them too. We were far apart but still under the same sky. That thought comforted me. *Moon*, I thought, *send us your blessing. Our plan has to succeed.*

We reached the sacred pool but didn't stop there. Instead, we pushed our way through thick undergrowth until we reached an ancient tree with silvery leaves. Its trunk was gnarled, twisted— and hollow. Sting slipped inside it and the rest of us followed. To my astonishment we came out the other side into a hidden clearing, surrounded by large boulders standing more or less in a circle. It looked a bit like a small temple without a roof.

We were still so close to the waterfall, I could hear the water splashing but it was also so cleverly secluded, no one would ever find it unless they knew exactly where it was.

'How do you know about this place?' Crow asked Sting.

Sting beamed at her proudly. 'This island holds no secrets from the leader of the Bee Children. Now let's start digging.'

'Are you sure no one will hear us?' asked Rain. 'We don't want to give this hiding place away.'

'I told you, everyone is too scared to come near the pool except the priests,' replied Sting, 'and I think only someone like Starlight would dare come here at night. But you're right. Perhaps one of us should act as lookout in case someone does approach.'

'Shadow will do it,' I said. 'He's an excellent lookout.'

I squeezed through the hollow tree and took my dog back to the pool. 'You stay here and keep watch, Shadow,' I instructed, rubbing the fur between his ears. 'Keep watch! Do you understand? Growl very loudly if you see anyone coming.'

Shadow thumped his tail on the ground to show he understood and I went back to my friends.

Sting had used the sharp edge of her digging stick to score a huge square in the secret hiding place. 'We'll need to dig a very deep hole,' she said. 'I reckon it needs to be at least the depth of a man standing on another's shoulders.'

We set to work at once. The night was so still, none of the shells and stones tinkled. It was humid in a way it never was back home. Insects buzzed constantly around our heads, occasionally swooping down to sting and bite.

With four pairs of hands hard at work, the pit was soon deep enough to satisfy Sting. She stood back from the edge, brushing damp soil away from her forehead. 'I bet not even a wild boar would be able to climb out of that,' she grinned. 'Now we need to cut down some tree branches. Not thick ones but not too thin either. And they need to have plenty of leaves on them.'

Rain held up a new knife Sting's father had given him.

'That's not sharp enough for branches,' said

Sting. 'I have something better.'

She pulled an axe from her belt and we took it in turns at hacking down branches. It was hard work, especially after all that digging in stony ground. My arms felt like they were going to fall off by the time we had covered the newly dug pit.

Suddenly we heard Shadow growl deep and long, and he came slinking up the path towards us. We barely had time to hide before a man and a boy appeared. They carried spears and had large bags slung over their shoulders. I held my breath and prayed they wouldn't stumble across our secret place. But they walked right past it without once looking round.

'I know those two,' explained Sting once they'd disappeared among the trees. 'Gull and Little Tree. They're father and son. Night-hunters! They're after hares and rabbits.'

'They're obviously not scared of the sacred pool,' said Crow.

'It would take more than tinkling shells to

keep Gull and Little Tree away from their nightly hunt,' giggled Sting. 'They're fearless.'

'Let's hope no one else has their courage,' said Rain. 'We don't want anyone to find the doorway in the tree and accidentally fall in the pit.'

'My mother gave me a charm to guard against that,' said Sting. She whipped out a bracelet of knucklebones that she pushed through the branches into the pit. 'Now let's get away fast,' she said. 'I think we should all get some sleep before it's time to carry out the next part of our plan.'

The second part of our plan involved me in an important role and, I have to admit, I was terrified I might fail and let my friends down. I prayed to the spirits and the Goddess to help me.

The next afternoon found me hidden in our secret place with Shadow beside me. A stiff breeze was making the stones and shells in the trees tinkle. I could hear Starlight and his men talking at the sacred pool. Their voices carried over the sound of the crashing water.

The sun started to set and, just like the day before, the priests departed, leaving Starlight alone to bathe. I heard their voices getting fainter as they walked away and I got to my feet. It was nearly time…

My heart was beating so loud, I was scared Starlight might hear it. My hand tightened around the bird-skull amulet. *Please, spirit of the long-dead healer, watch over me*, I thought. *Let this work.*

A moment later, I heard the loud call of a robin. It was a signal from Crow, who was keeping watch on Starlight closer to the sacred pool. Carefully, I emerged through the hollow tree trunk and stood right where Starlight would see me, Shadow panting at my feet.

'Bark, Shadow,' I hissed.

My dog obliged, letting out a series of sharp

howls followed by a long-drawn growl. Starlight, who was wading out of the pool, stopped dead in his tracks and looked up. He spotted me at once and his eyes narrowed with fury.

'You...'

I gave him a cheeky grin and a wave. Now that our plan had swung into action, I was actually enjoying myself.

'You impudent boy,' hissed Starlight, his face turning purple with anger. His shaved forehead shone.

I stood my ground as planned and the priest sprung towards me. He was surprisingly agile for an old man. But Sting and Crow had coached me well. I turned and ran back towards the secret place, Shadow scampering beside me. I could feel Starlight coming up behind us, getting closer. His arms reached out...

But then I dived through the hollow tree. Taken by surprise, Starlight stopped, but only for a brief moment. Then he came crashing through

the doorway after me. Once again, I was prepared. A moment before I reached the trap, I threw myself sideways. Caught unawares, Starlight kept on going and plunged straight through the branches into the pit.

I heard him roar in pain as he landed on stony ground.

Thank you, spirits, I whispered as I scrambled to my feet. *I am indebted to you.*

Rain and Sting emerged from their own hiding places.

'That priest can shout loud enough to wake the dead,' said Crow, hurrying into the secret hiding place. She walked up to the edge of the pit and looked down.

'Give me a hand up, girl!' growled Starlight.

'I'm obviously not strong enough to pull you out,' replied Crow sarcastically. 'Can't you see I'm only a feeble girl? But here's a friend who might help you.'

'Do you mean me?' said Rain, joining her at the edge of the pit. He looked down into the pit and sneered ferociously at Starlight. 'Greetings, sir. Do you still intend to offer me as sacrifice?'

Starlight shook his fist. 'I am not done with you yet. You shall—'

'I think we've had enough threats for today,' said Sting.

She indicated for us to step away from the pit. Reaching into her bag, she drew out a handful of yellow powder and blew it off her hand. A cloud of fine dust formed over the pit. The priest's eyes turned a bright red and he coughed violently as the powder settled on him. He tried to shout but only a stifled gasp came out of his mouth. Then he went limp and crashed to the ground.

'This powder works every time,' said Sting proudly. 'And there's nothing magical about it. It's just a mixture of ground plants and pollen. My grandmother taught me how to make it. Now, let's cover this hole up again. We don't want anyone to find the priest if they did accidentally stumble on our secret hiding place.'

Crow pointed to the sandals Starlight had left at the edge of the pool. 'We should take those and leave them somewhere far away from this spot. If the temple guards do go looking for him, they will lead them astray.'

Chapter 4
The Wild Boar

It was a long wait until night-time, when we were to carry out the next part of Sting's plan.

Sadly, waiting is not a game I'm good at. Time seems to slow down. I grow anxious. My fertile imagination makes up all kinds of stories about what can go wrong. I'm teaching myself how to keep my mind still and calm but it's not easy, especially when the stakes are so high.

At long last, the sun set and we hurried back to the secret hiding place. We carried two sturdy branches between us, with a sheet of strong, woven cloth hung between them. Sting also carried a rope wound around her right shoulder.

It was a breezy night, with the wind shaking the silvery leaves on the trees. The stones and shells around the lake were making an eerie clacking sound that sent shivers down my spine. No wonder people stayed away from this place. Were they the voices of the Goddess's servants? Were they angry spirits, warning us to keep away?

I kept telling myself that what we were doing was for the good of the island. Starlight was a bad man whose actions were putting people's lives in danger. We had a duty to stop him, and to save ourselves.

The chief priest was still out cold when we removed the branches, one hand tucked awkwardly behind his head. Sting secured one end of her rope to a nearby tree and shinnied down into the pit. She held her fingers to his lips. 'He's still breathing deeply,' she said. 'He'll be asleep for a long while yet.'

Looping the end of the rope under Starlight's arms, she looked up at us. 'Now pull him up gently.'

Crow, Rain and I pulled, Shadow wagging his tail furiously to spur us on. A limp body is extremely heavy, as we soon discovered, and progress was extremely slow. The three of us were all sweating by the time Starlight lay on the grass at our feet. Crow tossed the end of the rope back to Sting who climbed nimbly back out.

'Now we lay him out on the carrying poles,' she said. 'And we need to cover the pit again, just in case. We can come back later to fill it in.'

'It's a pity Starlight knows about this place now,' I said. 'If he tells the other priests about it, it'll be a secret no more.'

Shadow growled softly and we all froze.

'Someone's coming,' hissed Rain. 'Everyone, stand still. Crow, you go and find out what's happening.'

'I'll take Wolf with me,' whispered Crow.

We squeezed like shadows through the doorway in the ancient tree. Two of Starlight's men were at the edge of the pool, holding torches.

They peered round and we ducked behind a bush.

'Well he's not here,' said one of them.

'Where in the name of the Goddess could he be?' said the other. 'He's never missed an evening ritual before.'

'Perhaps he went down to the seashore,' replied the other priest. 'He often collects driftwood for the sacrificial fire. Let's alert the guards.'

On the other side of the pool, a loud squealing echoed out from among the trees. The branches of a bush shook wildly. The two priests stared at it in alarm.

'What… was that?' hissed one of them.

'I don't know,' replied the second, his voice husky with terror. 'Perhaps it's a messenger… from the Goddess.'

'Let's get away from here,' snapped the first priest. 'And make sure you don't step in the pool by mistake. The Goddess must be angry we've entered her secret place at night. She might put a curse on us if we muddy the water.'

Both priests turned on their heels and left. I have to admit, I was just as scared as they were. I'd never heard a more dreadful noise in all my life. And what was shaking that bush? Was it one of the spirits that protected the pool?

The squealing echoed again and something came crashing out of the bush. It wasn't a spirit. Before us stood an enormous boar; a wild pig with flaring nostrils and two deadly looking tusks. Crow and I stood rock-still as it grunted, peered around and came to the water's edge to drink.

I stared at it in disbelief. We'd received help not from the Goddess, but from a boar. Or perhaps the boar had actually been sent by the Goddess, to scare away the priests. In either case, we were rid of them. Once the boar had drunk enough, we could go on with our plan.

Chapter 5
Haunted Rock

I looked at Starlight lying on the ground. We had carried him all the way from the secret place to a desolate, foreboding shore. This side of the island seemed so different from the rest. The rocks around us were jagged; the kind of place people in my part of the world believed harboured evil spirits. There was a tree nearby that had obviously been struck by lightning. Its blackened branches stuck out at strange angles. They were festooned with deserted bird nests, their straw blowing in the breeze. A skiff was moored to it.

'My father left it for us,' explained Sting. 'It's a strong boat.'

'So where are we taking Starlight?' asked Rain.

Sting pointed to a small island on the horizon. Even in the gloom, I could see that it was shaped like an altar, with sloping sides and a flat top. There were no trees on it that I could see, no houses. Shadow whined, as if the place terrified him.

'We call it Haunted Rock,' explained Sting. 'It's said that's where the spirits of old went to live when people stopped believing in them. No one ever goes there because they think that if you came across one of the angry spirits, you would drop dead of fright.'

'What a terrible place,' I said, shivering.

Sting nodded. 'When there is a storm, you can hear the angry spirits howling from our island. The wind on Haunted Rock is so wild, sometimes the whole island shakes. Parts of it tumble into the sea. No one I know has gone there but it is said that enormous cracks have appeared in the ground. Should anyone be foolish enough to set foot on that place, the spirits will reach through the cracks and drag them into an abyss.'

'Oh you two, with your spooky stories!' Crow huffed. 'I doubt Starlight will drop dead at the sight of a spirit, whatever that may look like. It's only the perfect place to maroon him because it's on the opposite side of the island, away from the harbour where everyone moors their boats.'

Although Sting looked a little annoyed at Crow's dismissal of the spirits, she didn't rise to it. 'And if anyone *does* see him, they would assume *he* was an angry spirit. No one would dare go and save him. We'll let him stay there until the start of winter when you're safely back home. Then Father and I will row over and rescue him.'

'But aren't you scared the spirits might capture you?' I asked Sting.

Sting puffed up her chest. 'It will take more than a spirit to scare me.' She turned. 'Come on, let's get him into the boat. Crow and I will take him over and leave him on the shore. It'll be morning by the time he wakes up.'

'I sort of feel sorry for him,' I said as we dragged Starlight into the skiff.

'But he wants to kill us both,' said Rain.

You tried to kill me too but I forgave you, I wanted to say but I knew this was not the time to talk about revenge and forgiveness. We had no choice but to maroon Starlight on Haunted Rock if we were to escape unharmed.

'Father has left him a fishing rod and some furs in the skiff in case it gets cold,' said Sting. 'And I'm sure there'd be a stream for fresh water.'

'I hope so,' I said.

'I don't want

anyone's blood on my hands, not even Starlight's.'

Sting and Crow rowed the skiff over to Haunted Rock. Secretly, I was glad they hadn't insisted that I go with them. Sting might declare she was not scared of the spirits, and Crow didn't seem to believe in them, but I did. And I didn't want to run into an angry spirit. Rain and I watched as the skiff came back, moving quicker now that it was not weighed down with Starlight's sleeping body.

'Job done,' said Crow, mooring the skiff to the burnt tree.

'Now let's go move the boat Starlight arrived in,' said Sting. 'I know where it's hidden.'

CHAPTER 6
Back to Growling Island

Breeze the boatman had promised to come and fetch us in his boat in five days but, as it turned out, we had to wait for another five. There was a sudden summer storm, which apparently is quite common in this part of the world. The sea tossed and swirled angrily for what felt like an entire summer. Then, without warning, the wind died and the sun came out.

We filled in the time by shadowing Starlight's men closely as they searched for their leader all over the island. As expected, they didn't find him but they did come across his sandals, which Sting had left on the beach where they were bound to see them. They also found his boat gone.

We watched with relish as panic spread through Starlight's men. They must have assumed he had deserted them, escaping alone in the dead of night. Within a day, they too were gone, rowing away with their belongings piled high in their boats.

The night Breeze arrived, we had a lively gathering on the shore, organised by the Bee Children. It was their way of saying thank you for helping to get rid of Starlight. A lot of people came, to join in the dancing, to share food and to listen to the storyteller tell stories of the olden days. I hadn't realised there were so many people on the island, hidden away in valleys or making their homes in the caves along the rugged coastline.

'This island will be great again soon,' said Crow when the storyteller finished.

'It will take time,' replied Sting. 'We need to convince people from other lands that it is safe to come here again, to barter and perhaps set up home. But getting rid of Starlight and his men has proved to people that we can overcome obstacles, that we can mend that which is broken. It's given them hope. It's a new beginning for us.'

'I would love to stay and help you rebuild,' said Rain. 'I passed through many countries to get here, and I learnt a lot from what I saw. I could show you new ideas on how to build houses, how to clear fields and how to deal with enemies if you ever need to. But first, I must do the honourable thing. I must go to the sanctuary of the Whispering Stones and ask my father to forgive me for what I did to him and to Wolf.'

I looked at Rain proudly as he said that. He'd come a long way since we left Great Island. It was sad that we'd never had the chance to be friends before. If I thought about it, we had a lot of things in common. We were both hard-headed at times, we were both ambitious, and we both felt the need to prove ourselves to our friends and families.

I thought of his best friend Primrose, who he

never mentioned anymore. She'd travelled with him from Great Island but she hadn't come to the Island at the Centre of the World with him. I was almost sure they'd fallen out and she'd returned home but I didn't dare bring up the subject. I hoped that if they had quarrelled, they would make up again. Loyal friends are hard to come by.

'When I meet my father, I shall ask for his blessing to let me come back here—if you'll have me,' said Rain. 'I love this island. I'd love for it to be my new home. There is nothing for me on Great Island.'

'You will be welcome here,' Sting promised. 'You could live in our cave and help Father with his hunting and Mother with her farming.'

The day after the great gathering, Sting, her family and most of the Bee Children came to wave us off. 'The Goddess go with you,' called Sting as we pushed our boat away from the shore.

'And may she bless every step of your journey,' chorused the Bee Children.

Little by little, the Island at the Centre of the World grew smaller and smaller until it vanished in the afternoon haze.

'I can't wait to get back there,' said Rain. 'Imagine feeling the warm sun on your face every day and never having to shiver in the snow again.'

We reached Growling Island just after sunset the next day, docking at the same harbour we'd left ten days ago. Shadow barked happily and leapt onto dry land the moment he could. It seemed the entire village had come out to greet us. There were so many familiar faces and I was glad to see them all.

Eagle, a boy whose life we'd saved, pushed his way through the crowd, a welcoming grin on his face. 'Welcome back,' he said. 'We talked about you every day at home, praying the spirits will bring you back from the Island at the Centre of the World unharmed. You are invited to eat with us tonight. Mother has made her special sea-urchin stew.'

After our delicious meal, we all went for a walk. We were eager to show Rain the mine in Fire-Mountain, which towered above us and blotted out the stars. Its liquid fire-breath still glowed at its summit from the day it had erupted. I hoped it would never flow down the side of the mountain again.

Eagle told Rain the story of how Crow and I had saved the children trapped by the rivers of deadly fire-breath, how we'd led them out of the mountain through a maze of tunnels filled with choking smoke.

'That was very brave of you both,' he said, before grinning toothily and nudging me in the ribs. 'Especially for a twig like you, Wolf. Now, let's go and have a look at the tunnels.'

'I'm afraid the mine is not in use at the moment,' said Eagle. 'Father wants to make sure the mountain spirit is happy before we start digging for ochre again. We have left offerings, look: one for every child that was saved.'

Standing at the entrance, I could see lamps flickering in the walls.

'The spirit of the mountain *will* be pleased,' I said.

'Have you news of our friend, Ochre?' asked Crow. 'We were hoping to travel with him part of the way home.'

'I thought you might, and I made enquiries after Breeze left to fetch you,' replied Eagle. 'Ochre's parents expect him home in a few days. Mother said you can stay with us till he arrives.'

'That will be good,' I said. 'I think we all need a rest before the next part of our journey.'

'I'll go hunting while we're here,' said Crow. 'It'll be our contribution to your family's pot, Eagle.'

'I'll come with you,' said Rain. 'As I'm sure Wolf will tell you, I'm the best hunter on Great Island.'

I didn't offer to go hunting with them because the sight of blood still made me faint. I hate seeing animals dying, even though I know their meat is essential to keeping me strong and healthy.

Instead, I decided to explore a bit of Growling Island. With its grey jagged rocks and mountains, it had a very different kind of beauty from the Island at the Centre of the World. I wanted to see as much of it as I could. I wanted to make treasured memories I could take back home with me. Memories I could retell to the people in my village.

After supper the next day, when Crow and Rain set off hunting, I took Shadow for a long walk along the shore. Since the seeing dream, in which I'd watched the underwater monster dying and being reborn, I'd had little time to think about it. Now I had all the time in the world, and I sat down on the rocks to try and work out what it meant.

Who or what was the monster with long-reaching tentacles? Why had it died and why had the mysterious lights brought it back to life, stronger and seemingly more powerful than before?

I held the bird-skull amulet tight in my hands and racked my brains for a solution. But nothing came to me.

'It's useless, Shadow,' I said. 'The meaning of these seeing-dreams is beyond me.'

Shadow barked. I thought he was agreeing with me but then I realised something had caught his attention. I turned just in time to see a head disappearing behind a rock.

Someone was watching me.

CHAPTER 7
Azure

Who was following me and why were they hiding? Could it be one of the small children Crow and I had saved in Fire-Mountain? Perhaps they were hiding because they were too shy to come forward and speak.

'Hello?' I called.

There was no answer, but Shadow barked again and leapt at the rock, baring his teeth. I grabbed him and pulled him back. 'Shadow,' I said. 'What is it?'

A man emerged from behind the rock. At first, I could only see a tall figure that walked with a limp but, as he came out of the shadows, my heart turned to ice. The man was dressed in the robes of a priest. His hair was shaved at the front to expose his forehead and he had enormous hands. He was one of Starlight's men.

I took a step backwards, the hairs standing on the back of my neck. 'What do you want?' I said.

He smiled. 'Do not be alarmed. I am not here to harm you. My name is Azure.'

'I don't care what your name is,' I said. 'Stay away from me or I'll set my dog on you. He might look friendly but he's deadly when I order him.'

'I just want to talk to you,' replied the priest.

'But I don't want to talk to *you*,' I snapped.

'So go away and stop following us.'

I called Shadow to heel and we set off back to the village. I never once looked back to see if the priest was following me. Meeting him had shaken my very spirit. I'd never imagined I'd run into one of them on Growling Island.

Rain tried to shrug off the news when I told him and Crow what had happened. But I knew he was only pretending. If anything, he had even more reason to be scared of Starlight's priests than I.

'Perhaps you should stop going for walks on your own,' said Crow. 'Wait till Rain and I get back from the hunt and then we'll all go together.'

But evading the priest was not so easy. The next day, I offered to go looking for gull's eggs. They had gulls here too, although they were smaller than the ones on Great Island and their beaks were a different colour. I had almost a basketful when Shadow growled softly to warn me.

I glanced down from the rock I was scaling to

see the priest. He was standing at the edge of the water below me. This time he did not hide from me. In fact, he did not see me at first, or at least I didn't think he did. He was scooping water out of a rock pool and returning it to the sea.

Shadow barked, making the priest look up. He smiled when he saw me. 'Good day! I am rescuing the crabs. The poor creatures have been stranded by the tide. The gulls will get them if I don't return them to the sea.'

He smiled again and I noticed he had kind eyes that reminded me a bit of Moon.

'Your name is Wolf, isn't it?' he said.

I scowled, refusing to answer.

'You are considered a hero around these parts,' said the priest. 'Everyone talks about you. You and your friend saved the children from the anger of Fire-Mountain. Wolf is a fantastic name for someone who wants to be a powerful shaman.'

'I'm not interested in power,' I replied. 'I just want to be a shaman who helps people.'

I started to climb down from the rocks.

'Let me help you with those eggs,' said the priest. He stepped forward and took the basket from me while I clambered down the rocks.

Once I'd reached safety, I grabbed the basket back.

'I can understand your anger,' said the priest. Despite his kind eyes, I still couldn't get myself to call him by his first name. To say someone's name is to make friends with them, to accept their spirit into your life. I wanted nothing to do with this priest.

'What Starlight did was inexcusable,' he continued. 'Virtually kidnapping a boy in his efforts to try and wake She Who Sleeps. Shamans protect, not destroy. And then running away like that in the dead of night… It's something a coward would do, not a leader.'

I stayed silent, thinking of Starlight all alone on Haunted Rock.

'It is such a shame,' said the priest. 'She Who

Sleeps will never awaken now.'

'The people on the Island at the Centre of the World don't want the Goddess to wake up. They know she will be angry. They're just beginning to prosper again. Waking up the Goddess will destroy them once more,' I argued.

The priest shook his head slowly. 'The people of the island have got the story wrong. Have you not seen it happen before, perhaps in your own community? Something strange occurs that people do not fully understand. So they explain the parts they do not understand by filling them in with their own details, their own stories. Over time, the stories become facts, or at least things that everyone believes without question.'

My mind went back to Great Island. I thought about my adventure with the stolen spear. There, the people had definitely got their facts wrong. They had believed Rain without question when he accused Crow of stealing the spear. And, for shame, I had believed them as well. Only it turned out that we had all got it wrong. Crow hadn't stolen the spear. She was innocent. Innocent, and now my best friend!

Perhaps there was the slightest chance that the priest—Azure—was right. The people on the Island at the Centre of the World could have got the story wrong, just like I did with the stolen spear.

'The real reason we want to wake up She Who Sleeps,' continued Azure, 'is not to demand she make us into gods. We want to wake up the Goddess so that we can apologise, on behalf of our ancestors, for our vanity and foolishness.

'That will make the Goddess bless the island again. The trees will bear plentiful fruit once more. The islanders can come out and live in the open again, without fear of being cursed. Traders will return to the island anew. Does that not sound good, Wolf?'

He stopped talking for a moment and released another crab into the open sea.

'It is a shame that the only person in the world

who can help is going away.' He looked at me with his kind eyes. 'Only you, in the entire world, have the power to change things,' said Azure. 'Come back to the island and wake up the Goddess. I will teach you the spell you must recite. You are the red-haired child with the bird-skull amulet. The child of the prophecy. Starlight was right about you.'

The mention of Starlight's name was like a slap on my face. It brought me back to my senses. I could never think of that cruel, deceitful man—a man who was capable of sacrificing a child— doing anything for anyone's good but his own.

I grabbed the basket of eggs, making Shadow growl. 'I have to go now.'

But, on the way back to the village, I couldn't help wondering. Could I... have read *Azure* wrong?

'Don't be a fool,' said Crow when I told her about

my conversation with Azure that evening. 'I can't believe you even stopped to listen to the man.'

'You are too easily tricked, Wolf,' added Rain. 'Be careful, or it might be your downfall.'

Their words stung. Was I really easily fooled? Was I always trying to see the good in people even when it didn't exist?

After supper, I went out for another walk. This time, I found Azure sitting cross-legged on the beach.

'I see you are troubled,' he said. 'Perhaps your friends do not believe what you told them about the Goddess?'

I nodded and sat down beside him.

'To be a shaman is to walk a lonely path,' said Azure gently. 'No matter how close your friends are, they will never understand you fully. How could they? You have a connection with the hidden world that they do not. It makes you special but it also sets you apart from the rest.'

I remained silent, Shadow's fur brushing

against my leg.

'The ways of the Goddess are very mysterious,' said Azure. 'Think about it: if I am right about the ancient prophecy and the people on the Island at the Centre of the World are wrong, could you go back home without helping? Could you live with yourself knowing you could have saved an island from a great curse but didn't?'

I felt the bird-skull amulet under my tunic and thought about the last seeing-dream I'd had. Perhaps the dying monster was a symbol for Sting's island. The hordes of fish with sharp teeth were the curse. And the bluish-white light bringing the creature back to life was me, or rather my undoing of the terrible curse.

'But how can I be sure what you are telling me is true?' I asked.

'The Goddess will give you a sign,' replied Azure.

He picked up a piece of driftwood, crooked and worn smooth by the water.

'Oh you who sleeps,' he chanted, 'If you want Wolf to recite the ancient spell and wake you from your slumber, send him a sign.'

Azure threw the driftwood high in the air. It seemed to twitch and turn into a bird, which fluttered above my head for a few moments before soaring high in the night sky. Shadow, uncomfortable with the magic, whined.

'Was that sign enough to convince you?' said Azure.

I watched the bird growing smaller in the moonlight. My heart was in turmoil. The Goddess had obviously given me a sign, but what was I to do? If I was to be a shaman, I would have to make difficult decisions for others. I gritted my teeth, my decision made. 'I will come back to the island with you,' I said, 'but I must bring my friends with me.'

'Their doubt in your powers will only make your task more difficult,' Azure warned me. 'You will not wake up the Goddess if you have the slightest doubt in your mind.'

I stood up, dusting my fur tunic. 'I either come with my friends or not at all. I've disagreed with Crow before but she's always been there for me. She's saved my life more than once. I will not go without her.'

My words must have worn Azure down because he nodded wearily. 'Very well. Bring your friends. But hurry. We must leave at once. I have a boat waiting.'

CHAPTER 8
She Who Wakes

'You're mad, Wolf of Great Island,' said Crow. She'd been polishing her bronze sword when I came in but now she was holding it as if ready to use it. Her knuckles were white around the grip.

'I agree with her,' said Rain. 'You've taken leave of your senses.'

'Rain said it before and now I'll say it,' cut in Crow. 'That priest is tricking you. I never took you for a fool, Wolf.'

'But don't you see?' I argued. 'If there's the slightest chance of Azure's words being true, I just have to try and wake up the Goddess. I couldn't live with myself if I didn't help Sting and her people. Please, come with me.'

There was silence from both my friends.

'Very well,' I said. 'I'll fetch Azure. He'll explain it all to you."

I marched out of the house without looking back. Shadow followed closely at my heels. He was perfectly silent. I wondered what was going through his head. Did he agree with me or did he think Crow and Rain were right?

Azure was waiting on the shore, his eyes tightly closed as he prayed.

'They won't come,' I said miserably. 'They think you're playing a trick on me.'

Azure opened his eyes and shook his head sadly. 'This is your journey, and yours alone.'

'But if you speak to them,' I insisted, 'they'll see I'm right. That you're right.'

'It will be no use me talking to your friends,' said Azure sadly. 'There are some journeys a shaman must make alone.' He was silent for a moment, then looked directly into my eyes. 'Are you afraid of journeying alone? Because if you are, then the life of a shaman is not for you. Dare to act according to your heart, not your friends' advice. Dare to dream, Wolf. Only people who dare to dream have the power to change the world. Grasp the power with both hands. Dare to wake up the Goddess. Your friends will see you were right in the end.'

I looked at Azure, my mind a whirl of confusion. He was right. There are some journeys a shaman must make alone. Crow and now Rain were my trusted friends but there had always been a part of me that remained distant and hidden from them. The part of me they didn't understand—the part that made me a shaman.

I took a brave decision as I stood there on the shore with the waves lapping at the stones on the beach and Shadow still silent beside me.

'Let's go,' I said to Azure.

It took a while to get Shadow into the boat. He kept slipping out of my grasp and whining. But finally, we pulled away from the shore, both Azure and I paddling without speaking.

There's not much to tell about the journey back to the Island at the Centre of the World. The moon shone on the water, turning it silver. I saw dolphins some distance from the boat but I was too taken up with the mission ahead to enjoy watching their frolics.

By the time the Island at the Centre of the World came into view, I was exhausted. My arms felt like they would drop off at any moment. I was expecting to dock at the little harbour where we had said goodbye to Sting but Azure insisted we rowed round a headland and beached at a secluded bay covered almost entirely in dry seaweed.

'I can't wait to find Sting and tell her what we're going to do,' I said.

Azure fixed me with a hard stare. 'No one

on the island must know we're here. They'll try to stop us. Remember, you're asking them to change their minds about something they've believed for years. And they'll know soon enough what happened when the island starts to prosper. Meanwhile *no one* must see us. And make sure your dog doesn't bark and draw attention to us. Trust me on this, Wolf.'

We docked and climbed a dangerous pathway made smooth and slippery by many years of use. It led to the top of the cliffs where we found a wide plain covered in small bushes shining silver in the moonlight. Azure seemed to know the way. He had obviously used the path before. Before long, we reached the Forbidden Temple. It was deserted, the entrance completely unguarded. I remembered how scared the people on the island were of this temple, and I hoped they would stop fearing it once the Goddess was awake and the island prospered once more.

'Tie that dog outside the temple,' Azure ordered.

'He'll only get in the way during the ritual.'

'But Shadow goes everywhere with me,' I said.

'Just do as I say,' snapped Azure.

I obeyed, though with a heavy heart, and hurried after him down the corridor decorated with images of bulls, fattened pigs and geese. Lit only by faint moonlight, the creatures looked almost alive. They stared at me with sad eyes as if I was about to be sacrificed.

We came out into the circular room with the statue of She Who Sleeps and Azure struck a flint to light a torch. The statue lay on her side, one arm tucked under her head, her long skirt draped over her fat ankles. Azure's torch threw deep shadows across her face but I could see the eyes clearly. They were closed but I wondered if the Sleeping Goddess could see me just the same. Was she watching me from her invisible sleeping place?

For the first time since leaving Growling Island, I really feared whether I was doing the right thing. Could I really wake up the Goddess?

Could I, a small boy from an island at the edge of the world truly be the chosen one?

But there was no more time for hesitation.

'Help me light the lamps hanging from the ceiling,' said Azure, handing me a burning twig. 'Hurry up, it will be sunrise soon.'

With the lamps all lit, Azure hustled me into a side room and opened a large wooden chest. He pulled out two neatly folded robes, one for him and one for me.

Mine was the same one that Rain had worn during the first ceremony, with red spirals stitched all over it.

'Are you going to shave my head at the front?' I asked Azure.

'There is no time,' said Azure. 'I hope the Goddess will not be displeased when she sets eyes on you. Shaving our forehead is a sign of humility in her honour. Now, where's your bird-skull amulet?'

I arranged the amulet on my chest.

'Follow me,' said Azure, picking a hand drum

from the chest.

We returned to the circular chamber where Azure started humming an eerie tune. It sounded like a sad child crying far away, which filled me with sadness. Then the tune changed into a noisier, happier one and Azure danced around the Goddess, beating his hand drum.

'The hour is upon us,' he cried. 'The sun is rising.' He put down the drum and showered me with leaves from a basket.

As he spoke, a bolt of sunlight shone through a hole in the roof, wrapping She Who Sleeps in pearly light.

'Now, boy, now,' Azure urged me. 'Hold the bird-skull amulet up before the light of dawn passes from the room. Say the ancient spell.'

With trembling hands, I held up the amulet and breathlessly recited the spell. The sunlight shone on it, making the black eyes sparkle. I felt myself falling as if in one of my seeing dreams only this time I seemed to land in the same chamber as before.

Azure was still standing close to me. The statue of She Who Sleeps still lay in the sunlight.

The smoke from the lamps and torches filled the room. Through it, I could see the bird-skull amulet open its beak. Breath plumed out to form the image of a living bird, white as snow. It fluttered around in the sunbeam, scattering feathers that seemed to melt in the light. I knew at once this was the Goddess's sacred bird, come back to wake her up. It swooped down to the statue and disappeared into it, close to the heart.

A light, brighter than the sunbeam now fading from the chamber, shone from inside the statue. A ripple passed across her face. The hand on her chest fluttered and trembled. Her eyes gently opened.

I stood rooted to the spot with awe and wonder as, slowly, the Goddess drew her other hand from under her head and rose gracefully to her feet. For a moment, her gentle eyes fixed on me…

Then Azure leapt in the way, falling to his knees before the statue.

'Oh mighty mother, Goddess of Life,' he cried. 'I, your priest and worshipper, demand you grant me eternal life and let me stand beside you as a god! It is my wish and my right.'

No! I tried to cry out in horror but the sound stuck in my throat, and it was already too late. The kind look in the Goddess's eyes turned to one of absolute fury. Her mouth opened in a scream of fierce rage. She turned to Azure and her eyes fixed into his. The priest's hands flew to his chest and he clawed at his heart as if trying to tear it out.

A thunderclap echoed around the chamber and the whole temple shook. The shaft of light winked out, plunging us into darkness. I felt myself falling, to land back in the same chamber. The lamps were still flickering but Azure lay out cold at my feet.

And, slowly, the statue of the Goddess started to crack. It fell apart and, within moments, crumbled to dust.

CHAPTER 9
Anger of the Goddess

I stared at Azure on the ground. His face and hair were covered in dust.

I forced myself take a step towards him, to bend down and hold my fingers to his lips in search of a sign of life. He was dead.

I backed away from him, my scalp prickling all over with fear. The Goddess had killed him in her fury. And that's when my mind cleared and I realised what a terrible thing I had done. I'd let vanity get the better of me. I'd ignored my friends' warnings and chose to believe a stranger who'd lied to me.

'I'm sorry,' I shouted at the crumbled statue.

'I thought I was doing the right thing.' Then I turned and ran out of the temple.

With trembling hands, I untied Shadow. A sudden storm had blown up. The sky was a fierce storm of churning cloud. I ran blindly through the rain with no idea where I was going, Shadow's warm fur brushing against my ankles as he kept up with me.

On the edge of the woods, a familiar figure blocked my path. Sting!

'You traitor!' she spat. 'I saw you going into the forbidden temple with that priest. You tried to wake up She Who Sleeps.'

'I thought I'd be helping you and your island,' I screamed. 'I believed I was doing the right thing.'

'The right thing!' Sting spat at my feet. 'You have condemned the island to the Goddess's curse all over again. Well, now it's my turn to put a curse on *you*. You will suffer, Wolf of Great Island. You will suffer as my island suffers.'

I turned away from her without another word and ran. My mind was raging against Azure for betraying my trust but I also knew it wasn't all his fault. It was my fault too, for allowing myself to fall prey to his charms, for ignoring my friends' advice. I deserved Sting's curse. I'd let her, her family and her friends down. They would have to live with the Goddess's anger forever.

I have no idea how long I ran blindly in the rain, Shadow always beside me. I looked down at him and I marvelled that there was no accusing look in his eyes, just kindness and compassion.

My spirit was flooded with love for him. Shadow was my spirit guide. He'd always been there for me, and he was beside me now, in the darkest moment of my life. But where could he guide me to?

I had nowhere to go. I couldn't return home and try to help people after I'd condemned an entire island to a hopeless life of misery.

'Come on, Shadow,' I said when I came to the

bleak rocky shore with the lightning-struck tree. 'I know the only place where I can do no more harm.'

Chapter 10
Starlight Again

I searched along the coast until I found a battered old skiff abandoned at the foot of a cliff. I dragged it into water and climbed in, urging Shadow to follow.

Once he was sitting beside me, I started rowing through the churning sea. The wind howled around us, threatening to blow the skiff over. Shadow whimpered, his tail firmly between his legs. Poor thing, I knew how much he hated the sea after he'd nearly drowned in a storm near Great Island.

'We're not going far, Shadow,' I said.

The gloomy shape of Haunted Rock loomed

up through the driving rain. I rowed towards it, grunting with the effort. We reached a dismal beach full of jagged pebbles rolling around in the swell. I then grabbed a large rock and hurled it into the skiff, making a massive hole in it.

'There, Shadow,' I said. 'Now we're stuck here for good. We can never leave, even if I change my mind.'

The rain was still pelting down so I hunted round until I found a cave overlooking the sea. Shadow and I huddled inside it, shivering with the cold. I had nothing to make a fire with, nothing to eat or drink but I didn't care. I curled up among the rocks and went to sleep in my wet clothes.

I was woken up by the sound of Shadow barking furiously. Opening my eyes, I saw Starlight glaring down at me.

'Stay, Shadow,' I said, putting my arm around him. 'Let me deal with this.'

'You again,' hissed Starlight. His eyes were bright red, reminding me of the crab I'd once used as an amulet. Spittle dribbled down his chin. The hair at the front of his head was growing back. 'Where is your boat? I need it to get off this island.'

'There is no boat,' I said. 'I destroyed it.'

Starlight's lips curled in contempt. His eyes rolled back. It was obvious that being alone on this forsaken rock was taking its toll on him. He grabbed me by the tunic, making Shadow growl again. 'You lie,' he said. 'Where is your boat? Where are your friends?'

I wrenched my tunic out of his grasp. 'I came alone. And I sank the boat.'

'You came alone,' hissed Starlight. 'Why did you come? Have you come to kill me?'

'No,' I said. 'I've come here to stay… I woke up the Goddess.'

Starlight stared at me, a wild look replacing the anger in his eyes. 'Of course. You are the child of the prophecy—the Goddess has a way of guiding us all.'

'I wasn't guided,' I spat. 'Your conspirator, Azure, tricked me. He told me the Goddess would bless the island if I woke her up. But he jumped in and demanded she make him a god.'

'And did she?' asked Starlight, his eyes suddenly bright. 'Did the Goddess fill him with her power?'

'No,' I said. 'She struck him down dead.'

Starlight stared at me and let go off my tunic. 'I don't believe you.'

'I don't care if you do or not,' I muttered. 'He's dead. The Goddess will punish the island again, just like she did the first time the priests asked to be made gods.'

'But the wellbeing of an island is a small price to pay for becoming a god,' cackled Starlight. 'Don't you see? Despite its grand temples, the Island at the Centre of the World is a small, insignificant place, full of small insignificant people. So what if a few simple farmers and hunters have a terrible life? Those who are turned into gods will live on forever.'

'That is a terrible thing to say,' I cried. 'No one is insignificant.'

'You are a small person from a backward people,' sneered Starlight. 'Your horizons are limited by your lack of imagination.'

'My people are proud, loyal and kind. Look

at my friends. They tried to help me even when they knew I was being foolish. Your friend Azure, on the other hand, tried to become a god without you. He went behind your back and now you will never become a god yourself. The Goddess has destroyed the statue in the temple.'

'You lie, boy!' Starlight lunged at me and tried to haul me off my feet. I was shocked by his strength as he pushed me over and we rolled on the ground. I fought back, all the fear and anger coming through in my fists. But soon Starlight's mask of fury crumbled and bitterness was left in its place. He let go of me with a shove and sank down on the rocks beside me.

'We are alike, you and I,' he said when he'd regained his breath. 'We'd both betray our friends for power and glory.'

'You are wrong,' I gasped. 'We are not like each other at all. You are willing to betray your friends for power. I made a mistake. I did not betray my friends on purpose. I am not interested in power. I just wanted to be a shaman and now I cannot see how I can be one. I can't go back to my old life without my friends. I just want to be alone.'

'You are more of a fool than I thought,' growled Starlight. He stepped back and pointed two fingers at me. 'I will get off this rock one way or another and, when I do, I shall find another way to become a god.'

'Please yourself,' I said. 'As for me, this haunted rock is my home. I have nothing to go back to. I am cursed.'

CHAPTER 11
Visitors

I lost count of the days as I wandered around Haunted Rock, Shadow always beside me. After the storm cleared, a blazing sun shone out of a blue sky and the rocks underfoot gleamed like snow. Shiny-skinned lizards crawled out of their lairs to enjoy the heat. I noticed some of them seemed to have two tails, or at least a tail that forked in two like a snake's tongue. Shadow barked at them and once pounced on a green specimen that promptly scurried madly away, leaving one of its tails behind.

I felt sorry for the poor creature that reminded me of myself. I too had lost a vital part of myself.

There was no sign of Starlight although I kept a careful eye out for him. I was sure he was following me though, no doubt hoping I had lied about destroying my boat. On occasion, I could feel him close by, hiding behind a rock. Shadow would bare his teeth and growl and I would have to hold him tight. I hated Starlight but I didn't want my dog to harm him. I had enough guilt to contend with already.

I saw no spirits either. If they were on the island, they seemed to be keeping well out of sight. Perhaps they wanted no communication with someone who had proved to be a failure.

Wandering around the island, I discovered a clear spring with fresh, sweet water. I found flints to make fire so I could keep warm at night and cook. The rock pools on the shore were teeming with crabs and enormous shrimps. I had no desire for crabs, which reminded me of the old amulet I once had. I survived on the shrimps, and bitter wild berries that grew on thorny bushes. Once,

Shadow caught a plump, round bird and brought it to me fluttering in his jaws. I felt sorry for it and released it at once.

Every day, the moment I woke up, my mind was flooded with dark thoughts. I tried to shut it down, concentrating instead on finding food and fuel for the fire in my cave. Wood was very hard to come by on Haunted Rock and I learnt to make a fire by burning bird droppings and the dung of hares. It was better not to think. The image of the angry Goddess was still too fresh in my mind. I stopped praying to the spirits—what could I say in my defence? I was even tempted to throw away the bird-skull amulet, my last link with home and my calling, but something deep inside stopped me.

One clear night, I sat with Shadow on the edge of the cliff, looking out to sea. There was a light burning in a temple far away on the Island at the Centre of the World. I wondered how the people there were faring. Had the Goddess's anger started to take effect on them already? Was the island dying a second, unexpected death?

On perhaps my fourth or fifth night, it started to rain heavily again. I took shelter in my cave early, wishing I had a second, dry fur to wrap myself in. I stoked up the fire and sat close to it, steam rising from my damp clothes. Shadow, who was snuggled against me, pricked up his ears and barked. His tail flicked back and forth.

I thought he might have caught scent of a wild hare or some other tempting island creature close by. He sat up, growling softly and pattered out of the cave. I was too cold and tired to follow him. *He'll come back when he gets bored chasing whatever has caught his attention*, I thought.

He was gone for only a short while. I soon heard him barking again and he reappeared at the mouth of the cave. He wasn't alone. Crow, Rain and Sting were with him.

I was so surprised to see them, words failed me.

'Are you not inviting us in?' said Crow. 'If you haven't noticed, it's raining heavily out here.'

I indicated a place by the fire. 'Please, come in and sit. I'm afraid I have nothing to offer you.'

'Don't worry,' said Sting. 'We're not hungry.'

Crow sat down. I could tell from her eyes that she was relieved to see me but her mouth was still set in a straight light of anger.

'How… how did you find me?' I asked.

'When you didn't come back, Rain and I thought you were staying away because you were angry for not agreeing with you about Azure. And, when a day later, you still hadn't returned, we guessed you'd been stupid enough to travel with Azure alone.'

'So we borrowed a boat and followed you here,' concluded Rain.

'I told them about you waking up the Goddess,' said Sting. She didn't look directly at me as she spoke. I realised she was still furious with me, and I couldn't blame her.

'Is everything… fine on the island?' I asked hesitantly, dreading the answer.

'Nothing awful's happened yet,' replied Sting, still glaring into the fire. 'Hopefully nothing will. Maybe the Goddess decided not to punish the island again. After all it wasn't *our* fault someone tried to wake her.'

'No,' I said. 'It was my fault, for believing Azure.'

'We searched for you all over the island,' said Rain. 'No one had seen you. And then we met one of the Bee children, a fisherman's son, whose boat had gone missing. We guessed you might have stolen it and come here.'

I felt a pang of guilt at the mention of the boat. I'd never stolen anything before and I was aware that I had probably destroyed someone's livelihood.

Crow looked around the cave. 'Are you here to punish yourself for being foolish, for making a mistake?'

'I've put many people's lives in danger,' I replied.

'And this is the answer, is it?' snapped Crow. 'Running away and hiding.' She got to her feet, her dark eyes flashing with the anger I had seen so many times. 'I was disappointed that you did not heed my warning about the priest. But I am truly angry that you ran away from your own mistakes.'

'I am furious with you too,' snapped Sting. 'How dare you betray us after all the help the Bee Children gave you?'

'I can't apologise enough,' I murmured. 'I'm truly sorry.'

We all fell silent, staring into the fire that was slowly dying out.

'I am sorry for putting a curse on you,' said Sting after a while. 'I didn't really mean to. I was so angry—I just lashed out without thinking. I truly hope it doesn't come to pass.'

She reached out and put a hand on my shoulder. 'Let's forgive each other and be friends again. Come home with us.'

I thought of Sting's gentle parents. I thought of

the Bee Children, always eager to help. Perhaps they would find in their hearts to forgive me. I could go back.

But then I remembered the statue in the temple crumbling to dust and my spirit was filled with darkness again. It wasn't only the image of the Goddess I had shattered. I had destroyed my own life, my future.

I could never go back to my dream of being a shaman, knowing what a weak person I truly was.

'I can't come with you, I'm sorry,' I said decisively, stepping back from the fire into the shadows. 'Please go away. Shadow and I are remaining right here on Haunted Rock.'

CHAPTER 12
The Stone Knife

Time became meaningless. The sun grew hotter by the day as Shadow and I wandered around Haunted Rock, looking for food. It burnt my skin, which started to peel.

If I'm honest, I missed my friends—I was glad they had tried to rescue me—but I buried the hurt deep in my spirit. I was not yet ready to forgive myself.

Sometimes I thought I saw boats approaching across the sea but the images soon vanished with the summer haze. I realised I had started dreaming while I was awake. Or perhaps the blazing sun was playing tricks on my eyes. I feared I would

soon go mad like Starlight.

One night I was looking for gull eggs among the rocks when I spotted a brown bird, pecking in the moss for insects. It was an ungainly thing, with very small feet and a short beak.

'Poor thing,' I said to Shadow who was watching it intently. 'It's hardly equipped to find food or even walk.'

But presently the bird flew up with a fat, long worm dangling from its beak. It disappeared in a crevice high in the rocks where I heard the joyful twittering of hungry chicks.

'What do you know, Shadow?' I said. 'The bird might have a small beak but she's managing to feed her young just the same.'

My dog whined softly and, looking into his eyes, I realised he was trying to tell me something.

We may all be unsuited to the paths we choose but we overcome the obstacles by not giving up, by trying again and again.

'Oh, Shadow,' I said, hugging him. 'You are my guardian spirit.'

Brief as that moment of clarity was, it gave me new hope. Perhaps I *could* try to be a shaman again?

I reached into my tunic and clasped the bird-skull amulet again. For the first time since running out of the Forbidden Temple, I prayed to the spirits again.

'Can I be forgiven? Can I be the shaman I always wanted to be?'

The answer came a few days later. I was picking limpets on the shore when I saw a boat approaching. The hot sun was playing tricks on me again. But this time it was no trick. The boat came closer and Shadow wagged his tail and barked happily.

Crow, Rain and Sting had come back.

They moored the boat to a rock. 'We have come to take you away, whether you like it or not,' declared Crow, her hand firmly on the grip of her bronze sword.

'There is no shame in making mistakes,' said Rain. 'The spirits know I've made a few in my time.'

'What counts is how you deal with your mistakes,' added Sting. 'My father says it's what separates the brave from the cowardly.'

I looked at my friends and my spirit suddenly overflowed with happiness. Yes, I decided, I would go back and face the consequences of my mistakes. I didn't know how I was going to do it but I would ask for forgiveness from the people I had wronged. *The spirits give me strength*, I begged silently.

'Do you have anything in your cave you want to bring with you?' asked Crow.

'I have some food,' I said. 'It would be a shame to let it go to waste, and I need to put the fire out.'

We trooped up to the cave. When we returned

to the shore, Starlight was there, muttering angrily as he tried to untie the boat from its moorings.

'Hey,' shouted Crow and Sting at the same time.

Starlight looked up, panic showing in his eyes. 'Take me with you,' he begged. 'I am going mad on this rock. The spirits whisper in my ear all the time. I can't bear it any longer.'

'We brought you here to stop you chasing my friends,' replied Sting. 'And here you will stay until I come back to fetch you. But I *will* come and fetch you, I promise.'

'I beg you,' cried Starlight, tearing at his hair. 'I will not survive another night.'

To my great surprise, I found myself speaking up for Starlight. 'Perhaps we should take him with us. The statue of the Goddess is gone forever. He can cause no more harm.'

'I still say we should leave him here,' said Crow, slashing the moorings with her bronze sword. 'Just for a few more days until we get away safely. Then Sting can come and rescue him. I don't trust priests—especially not this one. He might have a plan, even if he looks weak and broken.'

'Please,' sobbed Starlight. 'Take me with you. Now!' He fumbled inside his robe and drew out a knife. 'Here! It's my payment for the ride.'

Crow's lips curled in contempt. 'I have no use for a flint knife, old man. I have a bronze sword.'

Starlight turned to me. 'You take it, then. It's not a flint knife. It's made of the same stone as the Whispering Stones. That should make it precious to you.'

I put my hands behind my back and shook my head. 'I'm sorry,' I said. 'I can't take it if my friends say no.'

'You are always bleating, "I'm sorry,"' scoffed Starlight, his broken look replaced by anger for a brief moment. 'Show some mettle. Order these women to take me with you.' He flung the knife in the boat. 'There, I've made my payment. You are duty bound to take me now.'

'Those rules don't work with me,' snapped Crow. She looked at Sting and me. 'Get in the boat and prepare to start paddling.'

Starlight lunged at the boat but Shadow sprang at him, barking furiously and baring his teeth. The priest fell back, kicking out and cursing, while the rest of us clambered on board. Shadow followed us in one leap, his fear of the sea seemingly forgotten in the moment.

'Row!' barked Crow as Starlight waded into the water, shaking his fists.

It was a bright, sunny day but a stiff wind was blowing in the right direction. It swept us away from Haunted Rock back towards the Island at the Centre of the World.

'You will go back and rescue him when we're gone, won't you?' I asked Sting as we neared the shore with the lightning-struck tree. 'He's a bad person but he won't last much longer on that desolate rock.'

Sting nodded. 'Of course I will, although I

shouldn't. His kind has brought so much grief to my island. He should be left there to rot.'

I spotted the stone knife at her feet. 'Oh look, we forgot to give him his knife back. You keep it, Sting. You can give it back to Starlight when you fetch him.'

Shadow sniffed at the knife, growling softly. 'Don't, Shadow,' I said. 'That blade is sharp. You might cut yourself.'

I bent over to snatch the knife away from him but the moment I touched it, strange voices started whispering in my head…

Chapter 13
The Vision

'*You were tricked,*' echoed a chorus of voices in my head. '*Tricked! You believed the priest.*'

'*Believed the trickster, the cheat.*'

'*And you woke up the Goddess. She was insulted once again.*'

'*Insulted once more.*'

'*A mortal wanting to be a god.*'

'*Trying to grab the power of the immortals.*'

'*That is why she cursed again.*'

'*A curse! A curse on the island.*'

'*A curse that will punish and destroy. Let the lesson be learned.*'

'*Let the mortals know! No mortal will ever*

have the power of the Goddess.'

'But the island was not cursed,' I wanted to scream. 'The Goddess has not punished.' My hand tightened involuntarily around the handle of the knife, made of the same stone as the Whispering Stones. When I'd touched the mysterious Whispering Stones at the Place of the Dead, they'd sent me a vision and now again I saw an island in my mind's eye, all green and lush with vegetation. A bright sun blazed in the sky. I saw fruit ripening on the branches of trees. Crops grew in the fields, lambs skipped in the grass. I heard people singing as they worked. Mothers sang. Children laughed joyously. I realised this was the Island at the Centre of the World at its best, a time soon to come...

And then the sky grew dark and the sunny island disappeared to be replaced by another one, a rocky, foreboding island with scenes of dread and horror. Through whirling snow, I saw people running out of their homes. I saw the wind tearing roofs off huts and homes. I heard children wailing. Wolves howled. The wind shrieked like a multitude of angry spirits.

'*They will be cursed,*' whispered the voices, jabbing at my head like bone needles.

'*Cursed!*'

'*The anger of the Goddess is coming.*'

'*Soon! It is coming. When the land grows stiff with cold and the sun weakens in the sky, the curse will come.*'

I saw a cave, deep and dark, glowing with hundreds of lamps. And I saw its roof collapse and snuff out the lights.

'*And it will last. The punishment will last for years.*'

'*Till the Goddess is angry no more.*'

'*Let them all perish. Let them all die. None should seek to trick the Goddess.*'

And then I saw a broken string of blue knucklebone beads fall and scatter on a dry floor. The knife slipped out of my hands into the sea. My eyes snapped open.

'We must go back home at once,' I gasped. 'It's not the Island at the Centre of the World that the Goddess has cursed. It's Great Island.'

Chapter 14
The Whispering Stones

I have a scant recollection of the long journey home. I do remember a tearful reunion with Sting's parents and me begging for forgiveness. I can still recall their blessing as we left the Island at the Centre of the World in a wicker boat, their parting gift of three bags of salt at my feet.

Back on Growling Island, we searched for Ochre and were lucky enough to find him preparing for another journey north to sell the precious red dust that had given him his name. We travelled with him along familiar country roads, now made hard underfoot by the long, dry summer.

We crossed into the homeland of another friend we had made on our way south. His name was Carver, because he was well-known for carving standing stones. I had been hoping we'd meet him but he had left the village a few days before. Here we said goodbye to Ochre who had reached his destination. We wished him good luck in selling his bags of coloured dust.

Carver had shown us a cave close to his village whose walls were decorated with pictures of dancing animals. Crow talked about it excitedly to Rain, making me smile despite the situation we were in. No one but me would know that she had not originally wanted to go.

'I shall go and see it on my way back to Sting's Island. Who knows, perhaps I could become a painter as well as a successful farmer and a brilliant hunter,' said Rain, wiggling his eyebrows at Crow to show he was only joking.

I was too worried about the situation back home to laugh at Rain's bigheadedness. Every moment I found myself alone, I begged the spirits for mercy. 'Do not let the curse begin before I get home,' I whispered out loud. 'Grant me the chance to save my people.'

Of course, I had no idea how I was going to save my people. Would the spirits come to the rescue at the last moment? Could I suddenly find a spell that would reverse the Goddess's curse?

I even begged the Goddess herself to forgive me, to punish me and me alone. If there was a reply, I did not hear it.

Three moons filled and waned as we trudged wearily on, stopping only to rest and eat the food Crow and Rain caught. Shadow, sensing my sadness, always stayed close to me. He would put his head on my lap whenever we stopped for a much-needed rest. His eyes would gaze into mine and his look reassured me. I knew he was telling me that everything would be alright and I tried very hard to believe him.

At last, we reached the very edge of Carver's

land. The sea lay blue and shimmering before us. It was a clear day and the white cliffs I had fallen off on the way south could be seen in the distance.

'We'll need to barter for a place on a boat,' said Crow.

'Thank the spirits we have the salt Sting's parents gave us,' added Rain.

We went off hunting along the shore for a boat and ran into Carver himself. He was talking to a boatman.

'Why, if it's not my two old friends from the north!' he said. He turned to me. 'You told me you were travelling to the Island at the Centre of the World. Did you get there? Are the famous temples as wonderful as they say?'

'Yes,' I said. 'They are as magnificent and majestic as the Whispering Stones themselves.' Though I didn't have the heart to tell him about the statue of the Goddess and how it had been destroyed. Perhaps he wouldn't have believed me if I did anyway.

We crossed the narrow strip of sea with Carver, docking at a small coastal village where we had made another friend. His name was Shell and we ran into him within a few moments of docking. He was incredibly pleased to see us, although he looked askance at Rain whom he knew had been my sworn enemy when we first met.

'Don't worry, Shell,' I said. 'Rain and I have sorted out our differences. We are friends now.'

Once again, we accepted an invitation to supper with Shell's family. The food was delicious but, in truth, I seemed to have lost my appetite. I felt too guilty about what I'd done to my island to enjoy anything anymore.

Crow showed our hosts her bronze sword, letting Shell and his father wield it. I tried joining in the conversation as much as I could, but my heart was not in it and I was glad when we finally stretched out under our furs to sleep.

Carver was travelling to the Whispering Stones again, where he was helping to carve new standing stones for the Place of the Dead. My heart grew heavier as we got nearer to the sanctuary. What was I going to tell Moon? I noticed that Rain was very quiet too.

'Are you looking forward to seeing your father again?' I asked.

He nodded thoughtfully. 'We have a lot to talk about. I just hope he can see that I am a changed man. I hope he will forgive me.'

'He will,' I assured him. 'Moon loves you very much.'

'What about you?' he said. 'Are you looking forward to meeting your mentor again? You promised you would bring me back and you succeeded. He will be proud of you, and grateful too.'

I thought hard before answering. 'I do not think I am ready to face him yet. How can I explain what I have done? Moon has put all his faith in me and I have let him down.'

'I agree with Wolf,' said Crow. 'I don't

believe in goddesses and curses but we shouldn't take any chances. Moon might still be weak and the bad news might affect him badly. Why don't Wolf and I continue our journey? You, Rain, can bring your father along at his own pace and we will meet you on Great Island.'

'That's a brilliant idea,' said Rain. 'It will also give me some special time with my father, just me and him.' He handed over the remaining salt. 'Take this. I'll see you back home.'

'Tell me something before you go,' I said, drawing him away from Crow. 'When you first accused Crow of stealing the sacred spear, you produced beads from the necklace my mother gave her to prove it was her. But when I found Crow, she still had the necklace. Where did you get the beads?'

Rain grinned sheepishly. 'That's an easy one. Your mother makes necklaces to barter, doesn't she? I spotted the necklace round Crow's shoulder and guessed it was a gift from your mother. So

I sneaked into your house and stole some spare beads.' He was silent for a moment. 'I am sorry for all the hurt I caused you, Wolf. I apologise.'

'I forgive you,' I said. 'But you must apologise to Crow too, for trying to make out she was a thief.'

'I already have,' he replied. 'Everything is good between us.'

He put his powerful arm gently around my shoulders. 'I must go. You take care, neighbour. I'll see you soon.'

I watched him depart with a sense of admiration. He was no longer the jealous boy who acted out angrily, not caring who he hurt. Now he was trying to mend those bonds he had severed and looked out for others. Not for the first time since we'd become friends, I hoped Moon would see the same change.

Chapter 15
Scattered Beads

More than two moon cycles passed before Crow, Shadow and I reached the cave where we'd hidden our skiff on the outward journey. I was relieved to see no one had found it, although it needed a thorough clean and some minor repairs. There were a few holes in the leather and mice had nibbled through some of the rope, but in a few hours we had it ready for the crossing.

It was late morning when we rowed away from the coast. Towards the afternoon, we spotted the Island of the Red Cliffs where I had once been taken prisoner. To our right, we could see fires burning on the coast of Seal Island, Crow's home.

'Do you want to stop there?' I asked. 'I could go on alone with Shadow.'

Crow shook her head. 'I will go on with you. If the curse does come true, you are going to need my help.'

'Thank you, Crow,' I stammered. 'I really am grateful for your friendship, and all that you do for me.'

For the first time in a long while, Crow really grinned. The dark cloud that had been hanging over the both of us since leaving the Island at the Centre of the World seemed to part, even if just for a moment.

'You're welcome, Wolf of Great Island,' she replied, clasping my shoulder. 'Though sometimes you do like to make it a challenge.'

We passed High Island where another of my friends lived—Sparrow. I hadn't seen him for a long time and I looked forward to the day we would meet again, but for now all my thoughts were on Great Island and my family.

Late afternoon saw us row past a rocky headland and the skiff was buffeted by strong waves that almost filled it with water. I looked across the sea to Great Island. Even from this distance, I could tell a snowstorm was raging. The outlines of the cliffs were blurred with snow. The few trees on top of them shook violently in the wind. My heart sank. The Goddess's curse was taking effect on Great Island already.

'I'll row,' shouted Crow. 'You bail us out.'

I had nothing to bail with except my bare hands. But I was so desperate, and I worked so furiously, I managed to keep the boat from sinking. Shadow was completely silent, sitting at the back of the skiff with his tail held out of the water.

The closer we got to Great Island, the rougher the sea became until it was tossing our skiff about as if it were an empty clamshell. At last, it hurled us into the waves and the skiff, free of its weight, went rolling across the sea.

I had been thrown into a raging sea before, so

I didn't panic. Instead, I grabbed hold of Shadow and paddled furiously with one arm. Crow burst out of the water beside me and we swam fiercely towards land.

A final wave sent me head over heels onto the shore where I landed painfully on my shoulder. Shadow landed close to me. He whimpered, then barked angrily and shook the water out of his coat. He licked my nose to reassure me he was unhurt.

'Good boy, Shadow,' I said, rubbing between his ears.

I looked round for Crow and saw her struggling to her feet in the waves. Her hair was plastered to her head.

Her face was turning blue with cold but she still held on grimly to her bow around her chest. She waded out of the water, gasping for breath.

'You two alright?' she called over the sound of the wind.

'Just about,' I replied. 'But I'm freezing. Even my eyelashes are frozen.'

'It's the wind,' said Crow, getting to her feet. 'Makes me wish I'd stayed on the Island at the Centre of the World.' She helped me up. 'Of course, if I had stayed there, I'd be sick of the sunshine by now and wishing for snow.'

We both peered around through the whirling snow. The beach was covered in a thick sheet of solid ice. Huge icicles dangled from the edges of boulders. I'd never seen anything like it.

'We'd better get inland,' said Crow, 'or we really will freeze to death.'

I have no idea how we managed to climb up the path to the top of the cliffs. My feet kept slipping on the ice and my wet clothes weighed me down. I was sure I was going to lose my footing any moment to be smashed to pieces on the beach below. When we reached the top of the cliffs, there was nothing but snow stretching out in front of us. It lay so thick, it came up to above my knees and got into my boots.

I hauled Shadow onto my shoulders and we battled our way towards my village. The snow got into my eyes, making it difficult to see but I knew the way by heart. We passed Moon's hut on the edge of the village, firmly shut and standing bravely against the storm.

Then I was stumbling blindly into the narrow, twisting lanes of my village. Shadow slipped off my shoulders and barked. No one answered his call. I wasn't surprised. Who would be out in terrifying weather like this? The howling wind was ripping the grass roofs off the houses. The middens, the rubbish piled up around the houses to keep them warm, had been blown completely away.

'Mother! Father! Hawk!' I called, lurching towards our house. 'I'm home!'

My hands trembled as I put my shoulder against the door to open it. There was no one inside. The house was empty. Snow was falling through the remnants of the roof.

All that was left was my mother's beads scattered across the floor.

Chapter 16
Primrose

'Wolf, you're back.'

I whirled round to see a girl standing in the doorway. I recognised her at once. Primrose! She really had come home without Rain then. Despite our troubled past, I was pleased to see her safe.

'Where's everybody? What happened here?' I asked.

'The snowstorm has been raging for many moons. No one can understand it, not without Moon to tell us why it's happening. It's driven everyone away.' She indicated a bag slung over her shoulder. 'I came back to see if there's anything I can take.'

'But where are my mother and family? Where's Hawk?' I said.

'They're all in the big cave near the lake. The whole island is there.'

'But they're not safe there either,' I cried, thinking of my vision. 'The cave will collapse in on them. We need to get them out of there.'

A great despair washed over me. I'd come home as fast as I could but I still hadn't thought about *how* I was going to save the island. I had no idea what to do next.

Crow, who had come in after me, searched around for two flints and lit a fire. 'Let's think about this,' she said.

'We need to get everyone off this island, away from the storm,' I insisted. 'The whispering voices told me it will last for years. But where can we go?'

'We could take your people to another island,' said Crow. 'My island! There's plenty of room for everyone.'

'That's a good idea,' I replied. 'But Seal Island is

too far away. We'll never get everyone there safely.'

'Then we'll take them to another one closer to Great Island,' said Crow. 'I discovered one myself during my travels. It's uninhabited and it has plenty of fertile land waiting to be cleared. Your people could start a new life there, or at least they can stay there until the Goddess stops being angry.'

Her words filled me with hope. 'Yes,' I cried. 'We could build new homes, away from the curse. But how do we get to this new island? How do we get all the people there safely?'

'We build boats,' said Crow. 'As many as we need. We'll row the people over family by family. There's only one problem: we have to walk right across Great Island to the other side.'

'Through the storm,' added Primrose. 'We have to walk through the storm.'

'The spirits will help us,' I replied, fired by my own enthusiasm. 'They will lead us to the new land.'

CHAPTER 17
The Wolf's Song

Crow and I followed Primrose through the falling snow to the cave by the lake. I remembered the lake well. Many moons ago, when the villages had thought I'd tried to poison Moon, I'd hidden in a small hut on a small island right in the middle of it. But I had never seen the cave. As we drew close, I realised with a heavy heart that it was the same one as the one in my vision. Shadow barked and ran in.

'Shadow!'

I recognised Hawk's voice and, a moment later, he came out. 'Brother! You're back. And you have brought your friend with you.'

Mother and Father stumbled out of the cave after him. I was shocked to see how much older they'd got while I was away. Mother's hair was going grey and Father had new wrinkles in his face.

'Son,' was all he said, for my father was a man of few words, but I could tell from his smile that he was pleased to see me. He bent to stroke Shadow's fur.

'Wolf!' Mother drew me into her furry cloak. I hugged her warmly and my heart nearly burst with comfort and happiness. She pulled me into the cave and the rest of the village gathered round.

'Wolf, you're back. Wolf, where is Moon? We need his advice.'

'Hopefully Moon is well and on his way home,' I said. 'But it will be a while before he gets here. Meanwhile, I have something to confess.'

I motioned for them to all sit down, trying hard not to tremble. My heart was beating in my chest like a drum. This was the moment I'd been dreading. But I also knew it was a moment I had to go through if I was ever going to find any peace.

'This island is under a curse,' I announced in a small, shaky voice. 'And I am partly to blame for it.'

An angry murmur rippled through the crowd. 'What did he say?'

'He's brought down a curse on our island?'

'But how?'

A sea of bewildered, accusing eyes turned to me.

'What did you do, second son of Bear?'

'Have you angered the spirits?'

'This boy's always causing trouble. He was never any good and never will be.'

Shadow, who could sense the anger in the crowd growled to protect me. Crow marched forward and stood proudly beside me.

'Wolf is a good and kind person. He is truly brave! What he did was out of foolishness not spite. It was a genuine mistake, made in an effort to help people. If he is as bad as you say, would he have come back to remedy the situation?'

'You're the one who stole our sacred spear,' shouted the rope maker. 'Why should we believe you?'

'Crow did not steal the spear,' I argued. 'She was framed by Rain. He'll tell you that himself when he gets home with Moon.'

'Meanwhile, you're all in grave danger,' added Crow. She turned to me. 'Tell them, Wolf.'

'First, we need to get out of this cave right away,' I said. 'I saw it in a seeing dream that the roof is going to collapse.'

Another murmur rippled through the people but this time it was not anger. This was fear.

'You lie, son of Bear,' shouted the rope maker. 'You pretend to have seeing visions so we'll recognise you as our new shaman when Moon is gone. But we never will…'

'But what if he's right?' came a voice from the back of the crowd. 'Should we just sit here and wait for the cave to crumble down on us?'

'The storm might last for years,' I said. 'But there is a way we can beat it. Our ancestors moved about the land, finding new and better places to settle. Now it is our turn to do the same. We shall move to a new island and start afresh.'

They stared at me as one and I knew I had their attention. I pointed at Crow. 'Crow knows of an island not far from our own that is suitable for our plans. We can get there in boats. We shall build them when we get to the coast on the other side of Great Island.'

'There is no time to lose,' I insisted. 'Those who want to come with us, gather your animals and your belongings. We shall meet near the burial mound and set out when the storm dies down a little.'

The snow had stopped falling and the wind was blowing less fiercely by the time we gathered outside the burial mound. It seemed, despite the protests, everyone had chosen to come.

A bright moon shone in the night sky. I took it as a blessing from my mentor and I raised my voice in prayer. 'We thank the spirits of the village for protecting us while we lived here. We thank the spirit of every house, every passageway, every stone and every hearth. We pay our respects to the dead we are leaving behind. We might be leaving but we carry our memories of you in our hearts wherever we go. We invite the good and protective spirits to come with us, to bless us again in our new home.'

I clutched the bird-skull amulet hanging round my neck and, talking in a private whisper, thanked the ancient healer who had gifted it to me.

'Wolf,' said my father who was standing close by. 'Should we not take the sacred spear with us? It has protected the village for many years. It will protect us on our journey and in our new home.'

'You're right,' I said. I called out a couple of men and together we opened the door to the burial mound. The last time I had been inside it, I'd shivered at the sight of the dead people around me. Now I had no time for fear. I approached the skeleton of the ancient healer and gently lifted the spear from his bony grasp.

'This will carry your spirit with us to our new home,' I said to the healer. 'When we are settled, I shall come back for you and lay you to rest in a new burial mound. I promise.'

Returning outside, I helped the men close the burial mound behind us. The people gasped when they saw the sacred spear, which I handed to my father. 'You should carry it,' I said. 'For in a way, you also protect this village, with your wisdom and strength.'

My father lifted the spear high above his head, and we all turned as one and started out on our journey. We trudged, family by family, across the frozen ground. Progress was slow but in the morning we stopped for a well-earned rest and a hastily eaten breakfast. A weak sun shone through the clouds and I urged everyone to hurry up. They obeyed me without too much protest. Crow, walking beside me, threw me a sideways glance as if to say, *see, they are starting to trust you.*

She was right and the feeling gave me new hope. Perhaps we would all safely get to our new land.

But, in the afternoon, the wind picked up again and, before we knew it, we were lost in a blinding snowstorm. Immediately, a ripple of suspicion ran through the crowd. People started to grumble loudly.

'How do we even know we're heading in the right direction, Bear?' I heard the rope maker ask my father. 'We might be wandering round in circles for all we know.'

'Just trust my son,' Mother answered.

Her faithful words filled me with confidence and I urged everyone to keep going. Until someone shouted above the sound of the wind.

'Look, haven't we passed by that strange, standing boulder before? We *are* going round in circles.'

'It's not the same stone,' said Crow. 'There are markers like that all along the road.'

'But it is,' said the rope maker. 'We're lost. We're all going to freeze to death.'

Crow turned to me, her tangle of hair covered in snow. 'Wolf, what should we do?'

I looked around at the frightened faces of my

people, waiting for me to answer. Somehow, I felt like the spirits were listening too, perhaps even the Goddess herself. I needed to do something, and I needed to do it now. So I would sing for them—all of them. Crow, my people, the spirits and even the Goddess. For she too was now part of my hidden world. I would sing my Wolfsong.

With the freezing wind lashing my face and my hands, my feet, my entire body going numb with cold, I threw back my head and started singing. Shadow joined me, howling loud and clear. The snow whirled around us, hiding Crow and all the other people from view. It almost looked like Shadow and I were alone but I knew we weren't. We were with our people, so I sang to the Goddess and the spirits about their families, their pets. I sang about their sadness at having to leave their homes, the only the world they knew. I sang about their hopes for the future, about their bravery in setting out to a new land.

And as I sang, something wonderful happened.

Wolves appeared out of the whirling snow, swirling around me like the tide surrounding a rock on the edge of the ocean. I could see their bright, kind eyes gleaming like fallen stars. Their thick fur brushed against me and I felt warmth return to my arms, my legs, my chest. I put my hand out and patted one of them on the head. It whined softly and nuzzled against me like Shadow does when he wants to petted.

The wolves all raised their heads to the sky and howled along with me, their song joined to mine. We drowned out the fierce sound of the wind, replacing it with a call for hope, for salvation.

These were no ordinary wolves. These were wolf-spirits, come to guide us safely through the snowstorm. On and on we trudged, without once stopping to rest or eat. No one wanted to disturb the awe and wonder of it all. Crow stared at me with admiration. I was always the one who had needed protection. But now I was the protector, leading her and my people to safety.

At last, the storm subsided. The wolf-spirits melted away in the snow.

I saw the shimmering sea ahead of us, glowing a bright orange under the setting sun.

'We've reached the coast,' said Crow. 'Thanks to your song and the wolves, we made it.'

Chapter 18
Wolf of New Island

I could sense a new respect for me as the people settled down on the beach for the night.

'Wolf, there are some caves further down the beach. Shall we shelter there for the night?'

'Wolf, the people are hungry. Most have run out of food. Shall we search for crabs and auk eggs?'

My heart filled with happiness as I answered their questions. This is what I had wanted all my life. To help and guide people. To be of use.

I had made good my terrible mistake.

My father talked to me with pride in his voice. 'Wolf, when shall we start building the boats?

We'll need to find a lot of driftwood. We'll have to make a lot of ropes.'

'You and Hawk are much better at these things than I ever could hope to be, Father,' I said. 'Why don't you take charge?'

It took ten days to build the boats, over a hundred of them. We could have built them in less but new storms kept blowing up and stopping us, forcing us to shelter in nearby caves. Sitting around the fire, I told everyone of my adventures with Crow and Rain, leaving nothing out; not even my mistakes, or my errors of judgements.

The crowd listened rapt, incredulous.

'Is there really an island that growls and a mountain that belches fire?'

'And a cave painted all over with dancing animals?'

'Did you really enter a grand temple with the image of... what did you call it? A goddess?'

'My brother is the first one of our island to travel right to the centre of the world,' boasted Hawk.

'I thought Seal Island was the centre of the world,' laughed someone. He turned to Crow. 'Isn't that true, chief's daughter?'

'I thought so too,' Crow said with a wry smile, 'but the world stretches far longer than we could have imagined.'

'Indeed,' I continued. 'The world is a vast place with many lands we know nothing about. There are people out there who have beliefs very different from our own, whose traditions are more advanced than ours. They use tools and weapons the likes of which we have yet to start using.' I turned to Crow. 'Show them.'

Crow drew out her bronze sword. The blade flashed in the firelight, making the crowd gasp.

'It's not stone,' she explained. 'It is made from the tears of two ancient spirits. They call it bronze, and it won't break.'

Some shook their heads in disbelief but others, bolder, reached out gingerly to feel the sharp edge of the sword that didn't break.

'People in other parts of the world use these kinds of weapons already, and they make other things out of bronze, like pots and beads,' explained Crow. 'We shall learn how to make them ourselves.'

Shadow sniffed at the sword himself and barked happily to tell everyone that he'd seen these things with his own eyes. Merry laughter rang out in the crowd.

We set off across the sea at dawn the next morning, after offering a sacrifice of food to the spirits. I wished Moon had been there to bless our impressive fleet. I missed my teacher and mentor more than I could tell, and I prayed to the spirits that I might see him again soon.

At last our new land came into view. Disembarking, we beheld a rocky beach covered in lush grass. Beyond it rose gentle hills, thick with trees and bushes.

Father drove the tip of the sacred spear deep in the ground. 'This will truly be a blessed home for us all,' he declared.

The crowd cheered and I led them on, thanking the spirits for leading us here safely. Personally, I also thanked Crow for discovering such a welcoming island.

The next few days were busy and happy ones. My father divided up the people in groups and allocated them all a piece of land. We set to building a new village very much like the one we'd left behind on Great Island but with bigger houses and wider passageways. We also chose a place for a new burial mound, with a clear view of the sea and the rising sun.

With everyone working hard, the houses and workshops went up in no time. The walkways were covered. Land was cleared for crops and pasture. Looking at the people, hearing their song as they worked, I wondered if they would ever miss our old island.

This new home was perfect in every way.

Crow took me aside the day my family moved into our new house. 'Wolf,' she said. 'It is time I returned to my own island.'

'Can you not stay?' I asked. 'Shadow and I will miss you. You have become a part of our lives.'

'And you have become a part of mine,' replied Crow. 'But I have a father who must be wondering if his daughter is still alive. I've been gone for so long. And my destiny lies on Seal Island. I am the chief's daughter and I will have to lead my people when the time comes. But my island is not so far away from your new one. I shall visit every year, and you and Shadow must visit too.'

'Yes,' I said. 'Our special bond will never be broken.'

Before Crow left, we organised a huge gathering in her honour. Everyone came to drink to her health and to sing the praises of the girl with the bronze sword. At dawn the next morning, she and I walked down to the beach alone. Father and Hawk had built her a new boat, lined with the best fur. Mother had made her a stew to warm her for the journey.

We hugged while Shadow howled mournfully. He had grown close to Crow too and sensed he would not see her again for a while.

'Goodbye, Crow,' I said. 'Thank you for all your help. I could not have survived all my adventures without you.'

'I wouldn't have missed them for anything,' she replied, picking up her oar. 'And it's never goodbye, Wolf of New Island. It's only "we'll meet again soon."'

Wolf of New Island! I liked that. A new name for me. 'Till we meet again, Crow of Seal Island,' I said. 'May the spirits guide you safely home, even if you don't believe in them.'

Shadow and I waved until Crow was no bigger than a small dot on the face of the sea and the light of the rising sun hid her from view.

Chapter 19
Comes the Shaman, Old and Young

A few days later, Shadow and I were looking for auk eggs when I saw a boat approaching. There were two people on it. One of them waved and called, 'Hello!'

I recognised that voice at once and Shadow barked joyously. It was Moon and Rain! I clambered down the rocks to meet them, rushing into the water to help drag the boat ashore.

'I don't believe my eyes. How did you two find us?' I asked, hugging them both. Shadow danced around us.

Moon looked healthier and stronger than I'd seen him last at the Whispering Stones. True, he'd lost more of his wispy hair and walked with a stoop but his eyes were clear. His hands trembled less.

'Father and I were on our way home,' said Rain. 'We've made up and he's forgiven me for all the horrible things I did. When we passed the headland at Red Cliff Island, we saw the snowstorm over Great Island. Father invoked the spirits and they guided us here.'

'Welcome to your new home,' I said proudly.

Moon looked around him. 'This is a beautiful place,' he said. 'And I can feel it in my weary bones that our people will prosper here.'

'We shall build you a new shaman's house,' I promised.

'Father would like that,' said Rain. 'But I myself am not staying long. I promised to bring Father safely home, and I have. Now I shall return to the Island at the Centre of the World. That is where I shall be happiest.'

Before long, word got round that Moon and Rain had returned. A great crowd gathered on the beach and the shaman was welcomed with open arms. Primrose shrieked with joy when she saw Rain and I wondered how she was going to feel when he told her he would be leaving again.

Mother invited Moon and Rain to our new house for supper—which still lacked a front door and a proper stone cupboard for her pots. We roasted a wild hare that Hawk had caught to celebrate. Moon brought my family a gift of wild berries. There was also a gift especially for me, wrapped in cloth. I unwrapped it slowly. It was a shaman's bowl, with a design of wolves dancing around the rim.

'Thank you, sir,' I whispered, touched that he'd remembered such a small thing.

'I told you I'd replace the one I broke,' he said with a smile. 'I made it while I was waiting for you at Sky and Earth's home.'

We ate and drank late into the night, laughing at old memories of Great Island; of our old home, gone but not forgotten. After the meal, Moon drew me aside.

'Thank you for bringing my son back to me,' he said. 'He's told me little bits of your adventures since you left Earth's house near the sanctuary of the Whispering Stones. But tell me the complete story.'

So I told Moon about the mysterious temple in the woods near the Whispering Stones and about Starlight and his plan to wake up the Goddess. I told him of the journeys with Carver and Ochre, about the Cave of the Dancing Animals and Fire-Mountain on Growling Island. I described every detail about the magnificent temples on the Island at the Centre of the World, about the Goddess and the visions and the seeing-dreams the bird-skull amulet gave me.

And I left no sordid detail out about my great mistake in returning to the Island at the Centre of the World, about my time on Haunted Rock. I spoke with sorrow, but also with pride about the vision that had made me return to Great Island, to find the curse of the Goddess had come true, and about the wolves that had guided us through the deadly snowstorms.

Moon listened without a word. When I finished, he got slowly to his shaky feet. 'Tell Bear to gather the people on the beach tonight. I have news to share.'

As the sun set, the people came. They brought hot food and drink, and warm furs to snuggle under. A great fire was lit and the children danced around it with their pets. The food was shared out and songs were sung, then Moon stood up and waved his shaman's stick for silence.

'It gives me great joy to see you all again,' he

said. 'And to see my son Rain home with me, if only for a short while. I have been on a long journey and I have learnt much along the way. But my young apprentice, Wolf, has been on an even longer journey, both physically and spiritually. You once knew him as the shy, hesitant boy who wasted time dreaming and fainted at the sight of blood.'

A murmur rippled through the crowd.

'But back then, I saw in him a tender spirit that wanted to reach out and help people. A kind spirit who deserved my guidance. He has told me all he has been through, his adventures out in the big wide world. I was waiting for a sign from him. And that sign came while I was away. I believe you all witnessed the appearance of the wolf-spirits who saved your lives? You all heard their wolf song. Wolves are animals of family and protect each other, like our Wolf has protected us. I think I have my sign, and I am ready for the next step on my own path.'

Moon indicated for me to stand up. 'Wolf,' he

said, 'I am old and my failing body yearns for rest. If you feel you are ready for the next path on your journey, then I hand over my duties to you. Will you comfort these people in their hour of need? Will you protect them and guide them?'

I knew the answer. In my heart, I knew I was ready. 'Yes,' I said simply.

Moon handed me his shaman's stick. 'Wolf, son of Bear, I declare you the new shaman. May the spirits guide your every decision.'

I have no words to describe my feelings as I held the shaman's stick for the first time. I caught sight of my parents and Hawk beaming at me, great pride lighting up their faces. Their pride filled me with humility and thankfulness for a loving family.

A brief hush fell on the crowd to mark the special moment. Then the children started cheering and the grown-ups followed. The celebrations went on late into the night.

Later, tucked up in bed at last, I took out the

bird-skull amulet. There seemed to be a glint in its eyes. The last seeing-dream I'd had came to mind and suddenly, I understood what it truly meant. The underwater creature was *me*. The fish with the sharp teeth were the challenges of life, tearing away flesh, draining their victim of hope and purpose. And the bluish-white lights were symbols of experience, breathing new life into a tired carcass.

The old, timid Wolf of Great Island was gone. In his place stood Wolf of New Island.

I felt happier at that moment than I ever had in my life. I thought of the Island at the Centre of the World and I knew instinctively that everything was alright there. The place was flourishing. Sting and her people were safe. And I also believed that Sting had kept her word and rescued Starlight from Haunted Rock. I liked to think that time alone on the little island had helped him change his ways. Perhaps, like me, he too was a new person.

Quietly, I stole out of the house with my beloved

Shadow at my side. We walked down to the shore in the moonlight and stood listening to the water lapping against the rocks. I closed my eyes and held tight the bird-skull amulet in both hands. With joy in my heart, I started to sing.

My Wolfsong was a new song, for a confident new shaman who was ready to face his future with all his skills and abilities. And it seemed to me that the foam on the waves formed a great pack of wolves and they danced to my song until the tide went out.

THE END.

AUTHOR'S NOTE

All stories are a journey! In some cases, as in the *Wolfsong* series, the journey is physical. Wolf, the hero, leaves his small village now known as Skara Brae. His travels take him to Stonehenge, through France and Italy and on to the distant island of Malta in the Mediterranean Sea. By the time he returns to the Orkney Islands, north of Scotland, he has seen some incredible sights. He has experienced things he would not have if he'd stayed back home.

But Wolf's real journey happens inside him, in his mind, his heart and his soul. He goes from being a frightened outcast who's terrified of the sight of blood to a decisive leader who saves his community. During his voyage he takes risks. He makes some bad decisions but his determination to stay true to himself and to do what's right brings his journey full circle with a satisfying outcome.

We all of us embark on a journey as the story of our life unfolds. The four *Wolfsong* stories might be set at the end of the Neolithic era but Wolf's journey mirrors my own at the end of the 20th century and the beginning of the 21st.

Like Wolf, I too was born in a small community where I felt misunderstood and unaccepted. For years, I had no idea what I wanted to do with my life. Only one thing satisfied me: telling stories. The people in my life, at my school, at home, did not think it was a talent was worth nurturing. Whoever made a living out of dreaming up stories?

So, like Wolf, I decided to embark on a journey of self-discovery. I wanted to find out if I was a good enough storyteller, if I could find my calling as an author. And I wanted to do it in the country where most of the stories I admired came from: England!

I upped sticks, gave up my job as a postman (I was just gone twenty by now) and left my village and my island of Malta with a mere £30 in my pocket. My journey took me to Spain, London, Brighton and finally Yorkshire where I settled in a house close to the sea.

Like Wolf, I had to struggle. I made mistakes. In London, I slept on the streets for a while (well, a park). I knocked on publishing doors that were slammed shut in my face. But I stayed true to my dream. And the gamble paid off. The dreamer from the village on the hill became an author, with books published in over 30 countries. My little story might not yet be all told, my circle is not complete, but I am where I always wanted to be.

As is the lot of most immigrants, I had to face some unpleasant hurdles: isolation, homesickness, racism (in my case, mild but still unmistakably there) and that horrible feeling that your contemporaries back home are advancing in their lives while you are stuck chasing an impossible dream. They set me back, they often dented my confidence, but they never killed my spirit.

So if there's anything you should take away from Wolf's stories, it's that no matter the cost, you should always follow your wish, your dream. You must listen to your heart and see where your journey will lead you. Society needs courageous dreamers and travellers. It needs people who can see beyond the hurdles other people impose on them. They are the true leaders of this world.

May you be one of them!

Saviour Pirotta
Scarborough, September 2021

DISCUSSION POINTS

Wolf learns how to take **responsibility** for his actions in *The Wolf's Song*.

- Why is learning to be responsible important?
- How does Wolf react to taking responsibility for his mistakes? Does he always do the right thing?
- Who is also responsible for some of the events in the story?

Wolf and Crow experience the mystery of **Skara Brae**, though this is a fictional portrayal.

- What do you think could have happened at Skara Brae to make the people leave?
- Some believe that Skara Brae was abandoned when the climate changed. Why do you think the people who lived there would need to leave because of this?
- Where else in the world has the climate changed the way people live?

Wolf struggles and learns to rise to the challenge of **leadership** in *The Wolf's Song*.
- Where do we see this most in the story?
- Are there any characters who help or hurt Wolf's path to leadership? How do they do this?
- Who are other leaders in the story? What kind of leaders are they?

All stories come to an end and Wolf's is no different. He finds **resolution** when he returns home to Great Island.
- In what ways does Wolf resolve parts of his life and journey?
- As readers, do we find a resolution in the story's end? Why or why not?
- How do you think Wolf's story could continue beyond this resolution?